The United States

Nebraska

Anne Welsbacher
ABDO & Daughters

visit us at
www.abdopub.com

Published by Abdo & Daughters, 4940 Viking Drive, Suite 622, Edina, Minnesota 55435.
Copyright © 1998 by Abdo Consulting Group, Inc., Pentagon Tower, P.O. Box 36036,
Minneapolis, Minnesota 55435 USA. International copyrights reserved in all countries. No
part of this book may be reproduced in any form without written permission from the
publisher.

Printed in the United States.

Cover and Interior Photo credits: Peter Arnold, Inc., SuperStock, Archive, Corbis-Bettmann

Edited by Lori Kinstad Pupeza
Contributing editor Brooke Henderson
Special thanks to our Checkerboard Kids—Kenny Abdo, Raymond Sherman, Peter Dumdei,
Annie O'Leary

All statistics taken from the 1990 census; The Rand McNally Discovery Atlas of The United
States.

Library of Congress Cataloging-in-Publication Data

Welsbacher, Anne, 1955-
        Nebraska / Anne Welsbacher.
        p.   cm. -- (United States)
        Includes index.
        Summary: Surveys the history, geography, and people of the state known as the
        "Cornhusker State."
        ISBN 1-56239-887-3
        1. Nebraska--Juvenile literature. [1. Nebraska.] I. Title. II. Series: United
        States (Series)
        F666.3.W45   1998
        978.2--dc21   97-27134
                                                                                 CIP
                                                                                 AC

Contents

Welcome to Nebraska

Nebraska is near the middle of the United States. It is very flat. Its name comes from the Native American word *nebrathka*. That means "flat water."

Long ago, strange, big animals roamed the Nebraska lands! Later, people used the land itself to build their houses. Through history, many famous people have been born in Nebraska.

Farmland covers almost all of Nebraska—more than in any other state. Corn grows on many of the farms. For this reason, Nebraska is called the Cornhusker State.

Opposite page: A corn field in Nebraska.

Fast Facts

*S*tate Flag

*G*oldenrod

*W*estern
Meadowlark

*C*ottonwood

NEBRASKA

Capital
Lincoln (191,972 people)
Area
76,639 square miles
(198,494 sq km)
Population
1,584,617 people
Rank: 36th
Statehood
March 1, 1867
(37th state admitted)
Principal rivers
Missouri River
Platte River
Highest point
In Kimball County;
5,426 feet (1,654 m)
Largest city
Omaha (335,795 people)
Motto
Equality before the law
Song
"Beautiful Nebraska"
Famous People
Fred Astaire, Willa Cather, Johnny
Carson, Henry Fonda, Gerald R.
Ford, Malcolm X

About Nebraska

The Cornhusker State

Detail area

Nebraska's abbreviation

Borders: west (Wyoming, Colorado), north (South Dakota), east (Iowa, Missouri), south (Kansas, Colorado)

Nature's Treasures

Two large rivers run through Nebraska, along with many smaller rivers. The Missouri River runs from the north to the south along the east **border** of Nebraska.

The Platte River runs all the way across the state, from the west to east. *Platte* is a French word. It means "flat."

Eastern Nebraska has rich soil. This land is good for farming. Western Nebraska has grassy plains. This land is good grazing lands for cows. The Badlands area has clay soil.

In the Sand Hills in western Nebraska, the soil is sandy. Grass grows in this soil. It keeps the sand from blowing away. In the 1930s, there was a bad **drought** in the Midwest United States. The drought caused dry soil to blow away.

Nebraskans learned to **conserve** water. They built dams to control the water flow in their rivers.

The Platte River

Beginnings

Native Americans first came to Nebraska about 10,000 years ago. In 1803, France sold the area now called Nebraska to the United States. Settlers began to move to the area. Many were **immigrants** who moved there to live and farm. People living in eastern states pushed Native Americans into Nebraska. Later, they forced Native Americans onto **reservations**.

There weren't many trees in Nebraska. Settlers built houses out of **sod** instead of wood. They cut chunks of sod out of the land and used them like bricks. They also dug under the sod and built houses like caves.

In the mid-1800s, southern states wanted to keep the right to own slaves. The northern states did not. People argued about whether or not new states should allow slavery. The Kansas-Nebraska Act was passed in 1854.

This act said that new states could decide for themselves whether or not to have slavery.

In 1867, Nebraska became the 37th state. In the late 1800s, more **immigrants** moved to Nebraska. Many people traveled west through Nebraska on trains like the Union Pacific. Farmers battled grasshoppers, **droughts**, and other hardships.

Farmers found new ways to bring water to their lands. This was called **irrigation**. Today, many Nebraskans have jobs in cities, but some still work on farms.

Drought during the 1930s left many farmers with nothing.

B.C. to 1600s

The First Nebraskans

8000 B.C.: The first Native Americans live in the area now called Nebraska.

1200: Natives are farming and trading furs and meat.

1500s and 1600s: Pawnee, Oto, Ponca, Omaha, and Iowa people live in Nebraska. Some move there because **immigrants** who live in the east are pushing Native Americans off of their land.

Nebraska

B.C. to 1600s

1700s to 1840s

Moving Along

 1700s: French fur trappers and settlers move into Nebraska.

 1804: The explorers Meriwether Lewis and William Clark travel to Nebraska.

 1840s: Many people move west along the Oregon Trail through Nebraska.

Nebraska

1700s to 1840s

15

1854 to 1970s

Statehood and Beyond

1854: The Kansas-Nebraska Act is passed. The law says states may decide whether or not to have slaves.

1867: Nebraska becomes the 37th state.

1870s: Large wars begin between Native Americans and white people.

1930s: **Droughts** and dust storms hurt the land, water, and farms.

1960s-1970s: More Nebraskans work in cities than in the country. Many build or sell machines for farming.

16

Nebraska

1854 to 1970s

Nebraska's People

There are about 1.6 million people in Nebraska. Many live in cities. Some live in **rural** areas. Throughout history, many leaders and famous people came from Nebraska.

Sioux leaders Crazy Horse and Red Cloud were from Nebraska. Both men led battles against the United States Army in defense of their lands.

Movie actors Marlon Brando and Nick Nolte were born in Omaha, Nebraska. Actor Henry Fonda was born in Grand Island, Nebraska. In one of his movies, *The Grapes of Wrath,* Fonda played a man living during the midwestern **droughts** in the 1930s.

Malcolm X, who fought for civil rights for African Americans, was born in Omaha. So was the dancer and actor Fred Astaire. Also from Omaha were baseball players Bob Gibson and Wade Boggs.

Mari Sandoz, who wrote children's books about Dakota people, was born in Sheridan County, Nebraska. C.W. Anderson, who wrote the Billy and Blaze series of books about horses, was from Wahoo, Nebraska.

Red Cloud (left)

Malcolm X

Henry Fonda

Nebraska's Cities

The largest city in Nebraska is Omaha. It is along the Missouri River. It has a children's museum. Trains come into Omaha.

Boys Town is near Omaha. It was a camp for boys who were poor or whose parents had died. A Hall of History tells about the history of the place.

The next largest city is Lincoln. It is the capital of Nebraska. It has a children's zoo and a museum of roller skating!

Other cities are Grand Island, Bellevue, North Platte, and Kearney. Kearney and North Platte have railroad museums.

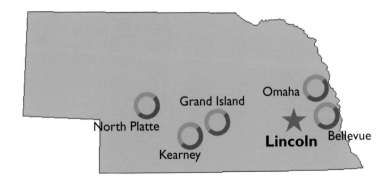

The State Capitol building in Lincoln, Nebraska.

Nebraska's Land

Nebraska's land is divided into three different regions. The Loess Hills and Plains form the state's biggest region. It covers the eastern and southern part of Nebraska. This region is filled with rolling hills, fertile cropland, and the Missouri River on the eastern **border** of the state.

In the far east and most of the northern part of the state is the High Plains region. Here you can find ridges and cliffs jutting high into the sky. The tallest point in the state is in this region. The Badlands extend into this region from South Dakota. These strangely shaped hills contain bones from dinosaurs and cavemen!

In the middle of the state is the Sand Hills region. This area is mostly hills that are covered with thick, long grass. Most of the land is used for cattle and sheep to graze.

Nebraska's land grows many different types of flowers. Violets, poppies, and wild roses grow throughout the state. Goldenrods and sunflowers are other pretty Nebraska flowers.

Bison grazing in one of Nebraska's National Parks.

Nebraskans at Play

Nebraskans love the rodeo! There are rodeos all through the state. In North Platte, the rodeo is part of a week-long June event called Nebraskaland Days.

The Cornhusker football team plays for cheering fans in Lincoln. Also in Lincoln is a museum with **fossils** and woolly-mammoth bones. Another museum, the Children's Museum in Omaha, is especially for kids!

Nebraska has many parks. It has two national forests and a large park filled with fossils. Arbor Lodge is a huge house with 52 rooms! Around the house are hundreds of trees and shrubs.

Opposite page: A rodeo in Nebraska.

Nebraskans at Work

Most Nebraskans work in service. People in service work at places like stores, restaurants, or banks. They sell farm things like seeds and machines. Nebraskans work as doctors, nurses, and lawyers.

Many people are teachers. There are so many teachers in Nebraska that one classroom has only about 14 students in it. So Nebraska kids can ask lots of questions!

Nebraskans also make things. They make foods, farm machines, and telephone parts.

Many Nebraskans still farm. They grow corn and raise cows and pigs. Others are miners. They mine oil, clay, and limestone out of the ground.

Opposite page: Farms cover almost all of Nebraska's land.

Fun Facts

•National Arbor Day was started in 1872 by a group in Nebraska City. Many people plant trees on National Arbor Day.

•Boys Town was founded by Father Edward Flanagan in Nebraska. The movie *Boys Town,* starring Spencer Tracy, was about the children's home in Omaha.

•A famous contest happens every year in Omaha. It is called the Logrolling National Championship. Two people stand facing each other on a log in a river and spin it with their feet. Each tries to make the other one fall off! The first logrolling contest was in 1898.

•In 1922, the largest mammoth **fossil** in the world was found in Nebraska. The mammoth was 13 feet (4 m) tall. The fossil is at a museum in Lincoln.

•The Cowboy Horse Race that began in Nebraska in 1893 was 1,000 miles (1,609 km) long! It took winner John Berry almost two weeks to ride from Chadron, Nebraska, to Chicago, Illinois.

•One of the largest swings in the world is in Roosevelt Park in Hebron, Nebraska. It is 32 feet (10 m) long and can hold 24 children!

•The Cornhuskers football team was once called the Bugeaters.

The Boys Town statue in Omaha, Nebraska.

Glossary

Border: the edge of something.

Conserve: to save.

Drought: a long period of time with no rain or snow.

Fossil: the remains of plants or animals that lived long ago.

Immigrant: a person who comes from another country.

Irrigation: a method of bringing water to where it is needed to water crops.

Reservation: an area of land set aside for Native Americans to live on.

Rural: the country, not the city.

Sod: thick, grassy land.

Internet Sites

Surf Nebraska
http://www.nebr.com/
Play STATMAN! Exclusive game for Husker Football Nuts!
Win a personally-signed Paul Fell "Husker Highlights" Cartoon!
Buy/Sell/Trade Tickets in the Flea Market and/or Talk Town.
Visit the Official Site for Husker Power. Talk about the '97 Orange Bowl.
Talk about the upcoming 1997 football season. What's the weather forecast for today's game?

Nebraska Game and Parks Commission
http://ngp.ngpc.state.ne.us/gp.html
This website gives you information on park & recreation areas, Nebraska wildlife, fishing information, boating, hunting, outdoor education, and much more.

These sites are subject to change. Go to your favorite search engine and type in Nebraska for more sites.

PASS IT ON

Tell Others Something Special About Your State

To educate readers around the country, pass on interesting tips, places to see, history, and little unknown facts about the state you live in. We want to hear from you!

To get posted on ABDO & Daughters website, e-mail us at "mystate@abdopub.com"

Index